D1777965

Drumcondra Branch

Lucinda Riley was born in Ireland. Her books have been translated into thirty-seven languages and sold forty million copies worldwide. Lucinda always used to tell her children there was a Guardian Angel watching over them.

Harry Whittaker is an award-winning radio presenter for the BBC and a member of one of the UK's most renowned improv troupes. Harry hopes to spread a little warmth through the Guardian Angels series, which he wrote with his mum, Lucinda.

Jane Ray is a children's illustrator admired worldwide for her exquisite, hand-painted artwork. She has illustrated over sixty children's books and been shortlisted six times for the Kate Greenaway Award. She has also won the Smarties Prize.

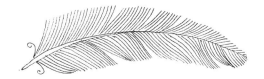

For Mum – Thank you for being my Guardian Angel on Earth – H.W.

For Rowan Thompson, with very much love – J.R.

First published 2022 by Macmillan Children's Books
an imprint of Pan Macmillan
The Smithson, 6 Briset Street, London EC1M 5NR
EU representative: Macmillan Publishers Ireland Limited,
1st Floor, The Liffey Trust Centre,
117-126 Sheriff Street Upper, Dublin 1, D01 YC43
Associated companies throughout the world
www.panmacmillan.com

ISBN: 978-1-5290-5119-3

Text copyright © Harry Whittaker and Lucinda Riley 2022
Illustrations copyright © Jane Ray 2022

Moral rights asserted.

The right of Harry Whittaker and Lucinda Riley to be identified as the author of this work, and the right of Jane Ray to be identified as the illustrator, has been asserted by them in accordance with the Copyright, Designs and Patents Act 1988.

All rights reserved. No part of this publication may be reproduced, stored in a retrieval system, or transmitted, in any form or by any means (electronic, mechanical, photocopying, recording or otherwise), without the prior written permission of the publisher.

1 3 5 7 9 8 6 4 2

A CIP catalogue record for this book is available from the British Library.

Printed in China

Lucinda Riley AND Harry Whittaker

BILL and the DREAM ANGEL

ILLUSTRATED BY
Jane Ray

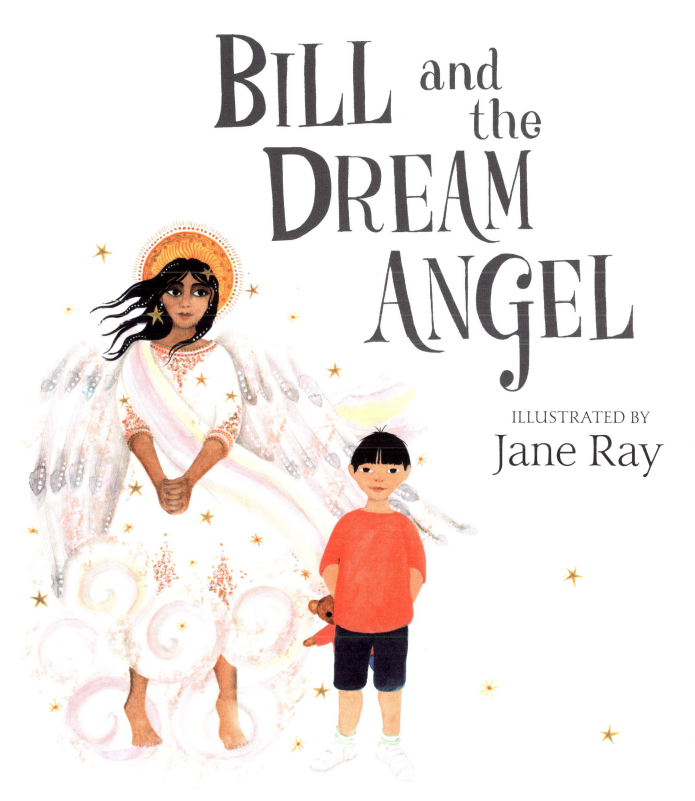

MACMILLAN CHILDREN'S BOOKS

If you are ever worried that something bad is going to happen, and your tummy and your legs feel like jelly, you can ask a Guardian Angel for help.

It's very easy to do, because Angels love to help people, more than they love anything else.

Angels are very old and very young at the same time. It sounds impossible, but it's not impossible to an Angel.

'Impossible' is just a word that humans use when they don't quite understand things.

Angels spend most of their time up in the sky, playing with clouds, arranging stars and watching sunsets.

But, if one hears you ask for help, the Angel will drift down to the ground, where humans spend most of their time.

This story is about a Guardian Angel called Destiny, and a little boy called Bill.

Bill and his family have just moved from a small flat in the town to a house in the countryside. Bill's mummy says that before their new home was a house, it was a barn which pigs lived in. Bill was a little worried when he heard this, because pigs are terrible snorers.

'Don't worry, Bill,' his mummy had smiled. 'The farmer has moved his pigs into a new home down the road. They won't keep you awake.'

Bill's new bedroom is much bigger than his old one. From his window, he looks out at the garden and the fields beyond, which stretch for miles and miles. All of Bill's things are in cardboard boxes. It takes a while to find Humphrey Bear, but eventually Bill does and puts him at the end of his bed, where he has always sat.

Bill knows exactly where his train set is though. It was the last thing he packed at his old home. He spends the afternoon building his biggest railway ever. It runs the whole way around his room, and he uses every single piece of track.

Later on, after Bill has eaten his tea and had a bath, his daddy scoops him up in his arms, and, being very careful not to tread on the train track, puts him into bed and tucks him in.

'Sweet dreams, Bill, see you in the morning,' Daddy says, before closing the door.

When we are sleepy, our thoughts start to run into each other, like streams flowing into an ocean that we begin to float on. Bill is just about to fall asleep, when he hears a sound.

Rat-a-tat-tat!

Bill wonders what the noise could be. It's a tapping that sounds a bit like rain, but the sun has been shining all day.

Rat-a-tat-tat!

Bill sits up.

Rat-a-tat-tat!

The tapping is coming from the window. Bill climbs out of bed and creeps over.

He gently pulls the curtains open.

There are a giant pair of shining eyes staring at him.

Bill runs as fast as he can and jumps back into bed. He pulls the covers tight over his head and wonders what on earth those eyes could belong to, and why they have decided to come to his bedroom window.

It must be a monster, Bill thinks.

He suddenly wishes very hard that he was back in the town. There were street lamps that stayed on all night, and he could hear people passing by outside. In the country, there are a lot more shadows and dark places to hide.

Bill decides that he feels safest staying absolutely still, hiding under his covers. If the monster can't see him moving, then it might get bored and go away.

After a while, Bill peeks his head over his duvet.

The room is very quiet.

It feels like his plan has worked.

Bill grabs Humphrey Bear from the bottom of the bed for some extra protection, and finally his eyes begin to close.

Soon Bill starts to dream.

In the dream everything feels a little ... wobbly. Bill can't find Humphrey, and as he looks around, he notices something odd about the two handles on his wardrobe.

They seem to be getting bigger and bigger. As they grow, they begin to change colour and shine, just like the eyes at Bill's window.

Bill watches as the eyes get larger and larger and closer and closer . . .

Suddenly, Bill wakes up with a big jump. It's morning, his room is light, and Humphrey Bear has fallen onto the floor.

Bill picks Humphrey up and squeezes him very hard. Then he slowly opens his bedroom door (just to make sure there isn't anything hiding outside) and walks downstairs for breakfast.

Bill's room

Bathroom

LOUNGE

'Good morning, Bill!' says Mummy. 'Did you enjoy sleeping in your new bedroom?'

Bill knows how excited his mummy is about moving to the countryside, and he doesn't want to frighten her by saying that there are monsters.

'Yes Mummy,' he replies.

'I knew you'd love it here! I thought that we might go and explore the fields today.'

Bill looks down at the floor.

'What's the matter, darling?' Mummy asks.

To keep her safe, Bill decides he has to tell Mummy about the monster he's seen. After all, it might live in the fields.

Mummy listens, smiles and shakes her head.

'Goodness! I promise there's no such thing as monsters, Bill,' she says kindly.

'How do you know, Mummy?' asks Bill. 'You've never lived in the countryside before. There were no monsters in the town. I want to go back.'

'Oh Bill,' says Mummy, 'I know it's different here, but in lots of good ways. You've got a big new room, and lots of space to play football in the garden.'

'BUT THERE ARE MONSTERS, MUMMY!' shouts Bill.

Mummy wraps her arms around him. 'Tell you what – why don't I come upstairs and help you unpack?' she says.

Bill spends the day setting out his toys and books with Mummy, and Daddy helps to hang Bill's big map of the world on the wall. By the time they are finished, it feels much more like his room.

But that night, when Bill climbs into bed, he starts to feel scared again.

His mummy gives him a kiss. 'Sleep tight, Bill. There's no such thing as monsters, I promise.'

After his bedroom door is closed, Bill scrunches his eyes shut and pulls the covers tight around him. He tries to remember lots of happy things, so there will be no room in his head for bad dreams about monsters.

Bill thinks about his friends from school, his favourite cartoon and even the chocolate cake he had for tea. He is just about to fall asleep, when he hears the sound.

Rat-a-tat-tat!

Bill sits upright in his bed. He looks towards the window and, through a crack in his curtains, sees one enormous, shining eye.

This time, Bill decides he won't even try to be brave. He does what any sensible little boy would do and runs straight down the corridor to Mummy and Daddy. Bill pulls the bedroom door open and jumps into their bed.

'Bill, what's wrong?' Daddy asks sleepily.

'I want to go home,' Bill says.

'But Bill, we *are* home!' says Mummy.

'No, we're not. I want to go back to our old flat. There's a monster in this house that gives me bad dreams. Please, take the monster away!'

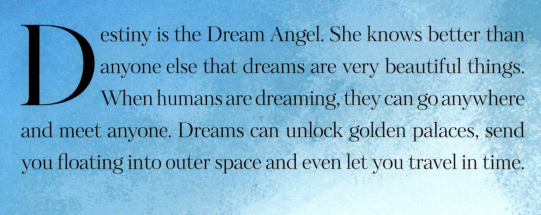

Destiny is the Dream Angel. She knows better than anyone else that dreams are very beautiful things. When humans are dreaming, they can go anywhere and meet anyone. Dreams can unlock golden palaces, send you floating into outer space and even let you travel in time.

But Destiny realises that not all dreams are good. They can be frightening, too.

If someone is having bad dreams, it is Destiny's job to stop them.

She begins to hear a little voice asking for help to take a bad dream away. (It is important to remember that even if your voice is quiet on the ground, it can still be heard by the Angels up in the sky.) The voice belongs to a boy called Bill.

Destiny jumps gently from cloud to cloud, until she eventually comes to rest on top of one right above Bill's house in the middle of the countryside.

She closes her eyes and listens again for Bill's voice.

'Please take the monster away.'

Destiny is wise enough to know that monsters only exist in people's minds. Sometimes, humans just need a little help to see things for what they really are.

Just above Bill's bedroom window, Destiny notices a small hole in the roof, and something moving about inside. When she realises what it is, she smiles, knowing exactly how to stop Bill's bad dreams.

However, Destiny will need some help from the farmer who lives down the road. In the blink of an eye, she travels to his cottage.

Remember, 'impossible' is not a word Angels understand.

As the farmer is climbing into bed, Destiny gently plants a picture in his mind.

That night, the farmer sleeps very peacefully, and dreams about some old friends who come to visit him every spring.

When he wakes the following morning, the farmer decides he should pay a visit to the family along the lane, who have just moved into the barn where he used to keep his pigs.

Bill hears a knock on the front door. When Daddy opens it, Bill sees a man wearing muddy wellington boots, and behind him, a big red tractor parked on the drive.

'Bill, come and meet our new neighbour!' says his daddy. 'This is Jeremy the farmer, who used to own this barn before it was turned into a house.'

'Hello, Bill!' says Jeremy. 'Welcome to the countryside. Now, may I ask who has the large bedroom at the top of the house?'

Bill's tummy does a backflip.

'Me,' he whispers.

'Well then, I have something to show you.'

Bill's knees begin to shake. Jeremy the farmer must know about the monster.

Jeremy looks at Bill's daddy. 'Is it alright if the three of us visit the attic above Bill's bedroom?'

Taking a very deep breath, Bill follows the farmer up to his room. Daddy opens the attic hatch and pulls down a set of stairs from inside.

Bill looks into the darkness. It seems like exactly the sort of place where the monster would be hiding. Jeremy doesn't seem frightened at all though, and is already climbing up the ladder.

'Come along, Bill!' he says, offering a hand to help him up.

Holding on tightly, Bill follows Jeremy into the attic, with Daddy climbing behind.

The farmer turns on his torch.

'Come and look over here in the corner,' says Jeremy.

Bill sees the enormous, shining eyes.

In fact, this time, he can see eight of them.

Bill turns around, wanting to run to his Daddy as quickly as he can.

'I just thought you might want to meet my friends,' Jeremy says, putting a gentle hand on Bill's shoulder.

Very slowly, Bill turns back. Suddenly, in the full light of the farmer's torch, Bill can see what the enormous eyes belong to.

They are not the eyes of a monster.

Behind the eyes are the fluffiest faces Bill has ever seen.

They belong to a beautiful owl and her three baby chicks. The owls have soft white bellies, with brown speckled feathers covering their wings.

'Hello again, Mummy Owl!' Jeremy says, before turning to Bill. 'I thought I should come and tell you that you might have some special guests staying with you here during the spring. This owl has nested in the roof of the barn for as long as I can remember, and every year she flies back to have her babies. She won't have noticed that it's a house for people now, not pigs!'

The little chicks cheep, and Mummy Owl spreads her long, downy wings in front of them. Bill thinks she looks frightened – about as frightened as Bill was when she was tapping at his window.

'She's just protecting her babies, that's all. We'll leave them alone now,' says Jeremy. 'You don't mind Mummy Owl coming to say hello to you now and then, whilst she's out catching worms, do you Bill?'

Bill says he doesn't at all. He thinks Mummy Owl and her babies are the most wonderful things he's ever seen.

That evening, as Bill is climbing into bed, he tells Humphrey Bear about Jeremy the farmer, who has promised Bill that he can have a ride on his big red tractor tomorrow.

Just as he is closing his eyes, Bill hears a familiar sound.

Rat-a-tat-tat!

Instead of putting his head under the covers, Bill goes straight to the window. He carefully opens his curtains and sees his new friend tapping on the glass with her beak.

'Goodnight, Mummy Owl,' he whispers.

She spreads her soft wings wide, and soars off into the night.

When Bill goes to sleep that night, he dreams of flying.

And somewhere, not very far away, Destiny the Dream Angel smiles down.